Z is

for Moose

BY KELLY BINGHAM

PICTURES BY PAUL O. ZELINSKY

Greenwillow Books, *An Imprint of* HarperCollins*Publishers*

Z Is for Moose
Text copyright © 2012 by Kelly Bingham
Illustrations copyright © 2012 by Paul O. Zelinsky
All rights reserved. Manufactured in China.
For information address HarperCollins Children's Books,
a division of HarperCollins Publishers,
10 East 53rd Street, New York, NY 10022.
www.harpercollinschildrens.com

Mixed media were used to prepare the full-color art.
The text type is Times Roman.

Library of Congress Cataloging-in-Publication Data

Bingham, Kelly L., (date).
Z is for Moose / by Kelly Bingham ; illustrations by Paul O. Zelinsky.
p. cm.
"Greenwillow Books."
Summary: Moose, terribly eager to play his part in
the alphabet book his friend Zebra is putting together,
then awfully disappointed when his letter passes,
behaves rather badly until Zebra finds a spot for him.
ISBN 978-0-06-079984-7 (trade bdg.) — ISBN 978-0-06-079985-4 (lib. bdg.)
[1. Alphabet—Fiction. 2. Moose—Fiction. 3. Zebras—Fiction.
4. Behavior—Fiction. 5. Books and reading—Fiction.
6. Humorous stories.] I. Zelinsky, Paul O., ill. II. Title.
PZ7.B51181685Zai 2012   [E]—dc22   2011002148

12 13 14 15 16 SCP 10 9 8 7 6 5 4 3 2 1
First Edition

 Greenwillow Books

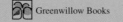

For Sam, who asked for a funny book,
and for Benny, because I love you too—K.B.

♥ is for Rachel—P. O. Z.

A is for Apple

B is for Ball

C is for Cat

E is for Elephant

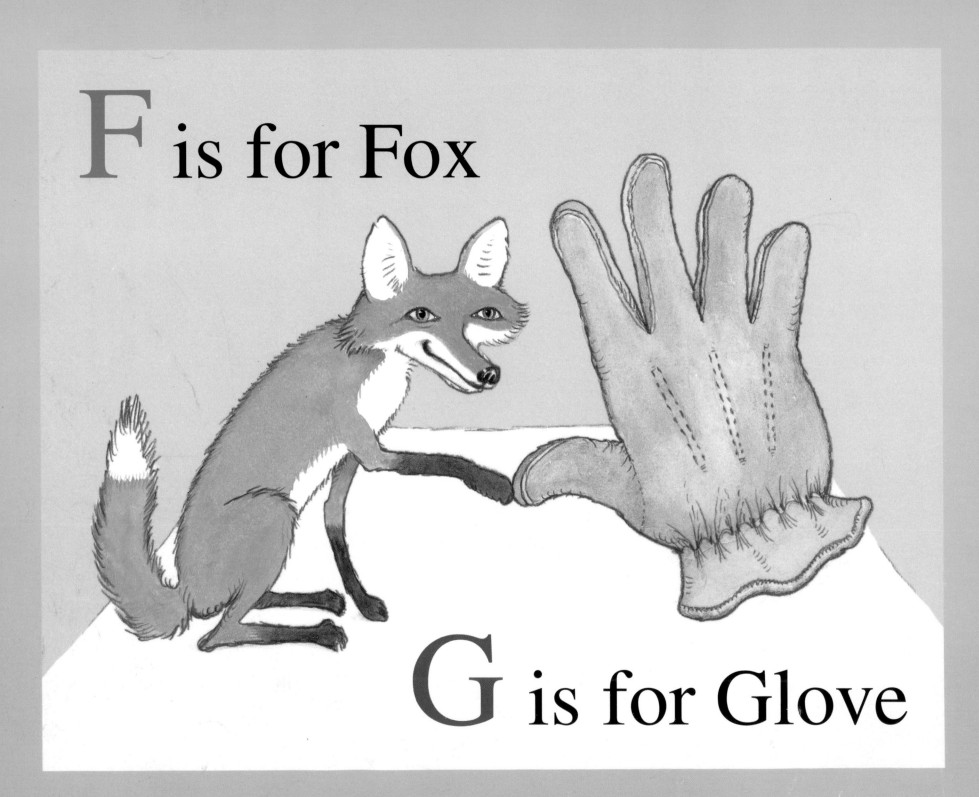

F is for Fox

G is for Glove

I is for Ice Cream

J is for Jar

K is for Kangaroo

L is for Lollipop

T is for Truck

U is for Umbrella

V is for Violin

W is for Whale

Z is for Zebra's friend, Moose

A B C D E F G H I J K L M N O P Q R S T U V W X Y Z

The End